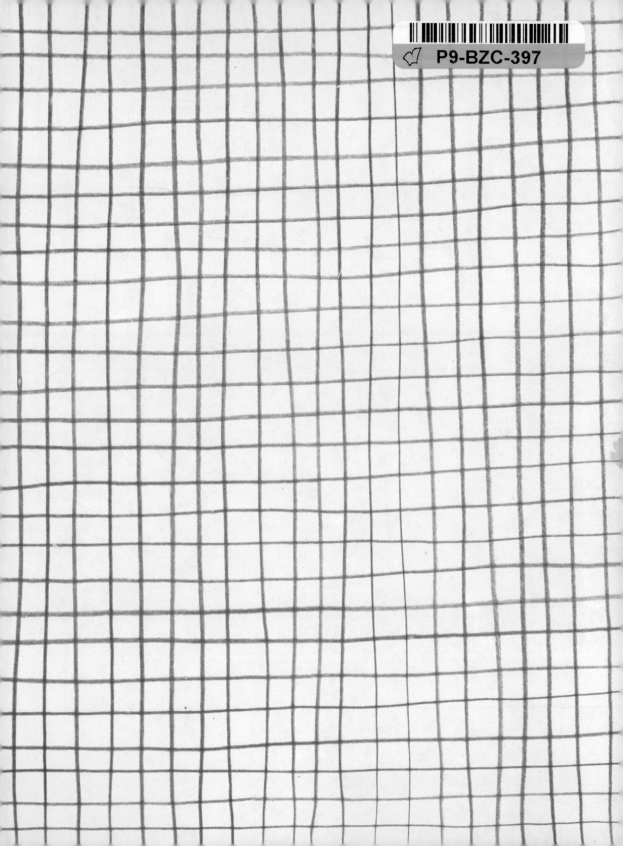

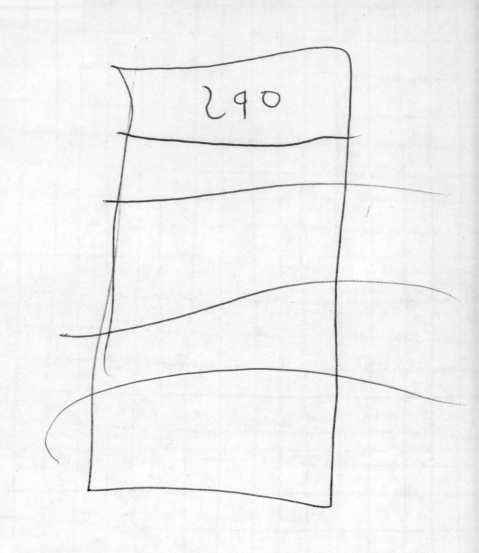

290

Weekly Reader Children's Book Club presents

A SECRET FOR GRANDMOTHER'S BIRTHDAY

by Franz Brandenberg · illustrated by Aliki

Greenwillow Books

A Division of William Morrow & Company, Inc. / New York

Edited for Weekly Reader Books and published by arrangement with
Greenwillow Books, William Morrow & Company, Inc.

Library of Congress Cataloging in Publication Data
Brandenberg, Franz, A secret for grandmother's birthday.
SUMMARY: A brother and sister cat plan the secret gifts
they will give grandmother cat for her birthday.
[1. Grandmothers—Fiction. 2. Birthdays—Fiction] I. Aliki. II. Title.
PZ7.B7364Se [E] 75-10606 ISBN 0-688-80012-2 ISBN 0-688-84012-4 lib. bdg.
ISBN 0-688-05781-0 (1985 Printing) ISBN 0-688-05782-9 lib. bdg. (1985 Printing)

for Yiayiá and Grossmutter

"I love visiting Grandmother," said Elizabeth.

"It's her birthday next month," said Edward. "What are you making for her?"

"It's a secret," replied Elizabeth.

"I love the smell of Grandmother's house," said Elizabeth.

"Are you making a lavender sachet for her birthday?" asked Edward.

"It's a secret," replied Elizabeth.

"I love Grandmother's apple cookies," said Elizabeth.

"Are you making potholders for her birthday?" asked Edward.

"It's a secret," replied Elizabeth.

"I love Grandmother's blueberry jam," said Elizabeth.

"Are you making a basket for her birthday?" asked Edward.

"It's a secret," replied Elizabeth.

"I love the way Grandmother spoils us," said Elizabeth.

"Are you making a fluffy pillow for her birthday?" asked Edward.

"It's a secret," replied Elizabeth.

"I love Grandmother's stories," said Elizabeth.

"Are you making a book end for her birthday?" asked Edward.

"It's a secret," replied Elizabeth.

"I love Grandmother's backrubs," said Elizabeth.

"Are you making a soap dish for her birthday?" asked Edward.

"It's a secret," replied Elizabeth.

"I love it when Grandmother lets us stay up late," said Elizabeth.

"Are you making a lamp shade for her birthday?" asked Edward.

"It's a secret," replied Elizabeth.

"I love Grandmother's pretty pink apron", said Elizabeth.

"Are you making pink wrapping paper for her birthday?" asked Edward.

"It's a secret", replied Elizabeth.

"I love how Grandmother combs out her long, white hair at night," said Elizabeth.

"Are you knitting a headband for her birthday?" asked Edward.

"It's a secret," replied Elizabeth.

"What are you making Grandmother for her birthday?" asked Elizabeth.

"It's a secret," replied Edward.

For her birthday, Elizabeth gave
Grandmother a lavender sachet,
a pair of potholders, a basket,
a fluffy pillow, a book end,
a soap dish, a lamp shade, wrapping
paper and a knitted headband.

Grandmother hugged and kissed her.
She had tears in her eyes.

"I made everything myself, Grandma,"
said Elizabeth.

"I have a poem for your birthday, Grandma," said Edward. "Here it is."

We love visiting you, Grandma.
We love the smell of your house, Grandma.
Grandma, we love your apple cookies.
Grandma, we love your blueberry jam.
We love the way you spoil us, Grandma.
We love your stories, Grandma.
Grandma, we love your backrubs.
Grandma, we love it when you let us stay up late.
We love your pretty pink apron, Grandma.
We love how you comb out your long, white hair
*   at night, Grandma.*
But especially, we love you, Grandma.
Happy birthday, dear Grandma,
*   happy birthday to you.*

Grandmother hugged and kissed him. She had tears in her eyes.

"I wrote it all by myself, Grandma," said Edward.

"This is my happiest birthday,"
said Grandmother.

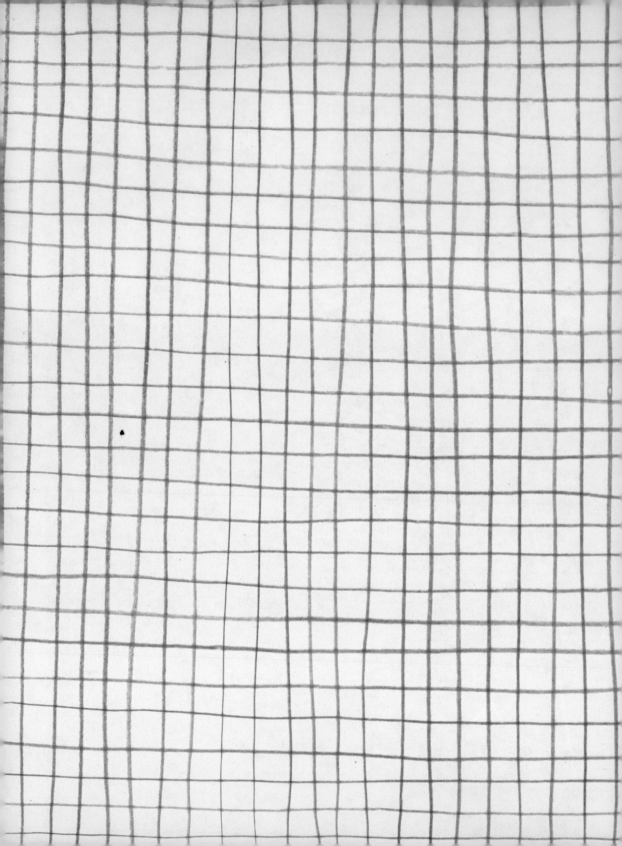